3 Fun-to-Read-Aloud Stories With a Message

SPORTS STORIES

The Standard Publishing Company, Cincinnati, Ohio
A division of Standex International Corporation

Printed in the United States of America

07 06 05 04 03 02 01 00 5 4 3 2 1

Library of Congress Catalog Card Number 98-061461
ISBN 0-7847-0819-3

THE PENGUINS' BIG WIN

written by Clare Mishica
illustrated by Terri Steiger

Bzzzz! rang the buzzer.

"We are number one!" cheered the Eagles.

The Penguins did not cheer. They had lost the hockey game. "We will win next time," said Andy.

But at the next game, Tami and Andy fell down five times. Carlos skated into the net. Jamal and Kristen lost their hockey sticks. And Brian made a goal for the other team. The Penguins did not win.

"I know how to win," said Andy. "I have a plan."

"What is it?" asked Brian. "What should we do?"

"Everyone should bring something lucky to the next game," said Andy. "Then we will win."

Before the next game, Brian put a lucky penny in his skate. Tami and Kristen wore their lucky socks. Jamal wore his lucky jersey. Carlos put his lucky marble in his pocket. Andy wore his lucky hat under his helmet.

Bzzzz! The game began. Andy skated onto the ice. His lucky hat slipped down over his eyes. Andy skated right into Kristen. Kristen fell down. She dropped her hockey stick. Jamal tripped over it. Then Brian and Carlos tripped over Jamal. Andy's plan did not work.

The Penguins lost the game. And they lost the next game, and the next game.

"We will keep trying," Coach told the Penguins. "We have three games left."

"We will never win," said Andy. "Kristen keeps dropping her hockey stick."

"It is not me," said Kristen. "Carlos skates into everyone."

"It is not me," said Carlos. "Jamal gets too many penalties."

"It is not me," said Jamal. "Brian shoots the puck into the wrong net."

"It is not me," said Brian. "Tami and Andy cannot stand up."

"Stop!" said Coach. "We will not win this way. But I have a plan. Wait right here."

The Penguins waited for Coach. "I can guess Coach's plan," said Andy. "He will tell all of you to pass me the puck and let me score."

"No way," said Carlos. "You would fall on the puck. Coach will say to pass it to me."

"Not you," said Tami. "You would skate right over it."

Coach came back with a hat in his hand. There were papers in the hat. "Is that our plan?" asked Andy.

"It is part of my plan," said Coach. "I want each of you to write a letter."

Brian scraped up a pile of icy snow with his skate blade. "Who to?" he asked.

Coach held out his hat. "Everyone pick a paper from my hat," he said. "Write a letter to the Penguin whose name is on the paper."

Kristen skated a figure eight.

"What should we write about?" she asked.

"Tell that person what he or she does best," said Coach.

"Do we have to?" asked Carlos, shooting a puck down the ice.

"Yes," said Coach. "It is part of my plan. Bring me the letters tomorrow."

The Penguins brought their letters to Coach the next day. "Now tell us your plan before the game starts," said Jamal.

Coach put his arm on Jamal's shoulder. "First, I must read the letters," Coach said. "Everyone sit down and listen."

"Do we have to?" asked Brian.

"Yes," said Coach. "It is part of my plan."

Coach opened a letter. "Dear Andy," he read, "You can stop the puck good." Andy smiled. I will stop even better today, he thought.

Then Coach read, "Dear Kristen, You pass the puck the very best." Kristen put on her knee pads. I will pass the puck even better today, she thought.

The next letter said, "Dear Brian, You are good at putting the puck into the net." Brian tied up his skates. I will put the puck into the right net today, he thought.

Then Coach read, "Dear Jamal, You make good penalty shots." I will make every shot today, thought Jamal.

Then Coach read, "Dear Carlos, You are a fast skater." Carlos put on his helmet. I will skate even faster today, he thought.

The last letter said, "Dear Tami, You are a good goalie." Tami picked up her hockey stick. I will be the best goalie today, she thought.

Bzzzz! The buzzer rang. "Let's go!" said Coach.

"But what is the plan?" said Brian.

"I will tell you later," said Coach.

The Penguins skated out on the ice. The Eagles skated out on the ice. Bzzzz! rang the buzzer. Swoosh! went the puck.

Kristen passed the puck to Carlos. Carlos skated down the ice very fast. He passed the puck to Andy. Andy skated near the net. He stopped. He passed the puck to Brian. Brian shot the puck. It went into the net!

"All right!" cheered the Penguins. They had one goal.

The Penguins played better than ever before. Tami did not let the Eagles score. The Penguins won the game 2 to 0. The Penguins cheered. "Good game!" said Coach. He gave everyone a high five.

"I guess we do not need to know your plan now," said Tami.

Coach smiled. "But you do know it," he said. "My plan is what the apostle Paul wrote in the Bible," said Coach. "Paul told people to encourage one another and build each other up."

"We encouraged each other with our letters!" said Andy.

"Coach's plan worked!" said Tami.

"You are the smartest coach!" said Jamal.

"Yeah for Coach!" cheered the Penguins, and everyone hugged Coach.

"Thank you for encouraging me," Coach said.

"If we always encourage each other," said Kristen, "we will always be winners."

"Yes," said Carlos. "Then we will be winners even if we lose the game."

MARTY'S MONSTER

written by Nancy Ellen Hird
illustrated by Valerie Damon

Soccer practice was over. Marty walked right past her friend Robin. "Marty, wait!" called Robin. "We always walk home together." Marty stopped. "What a good practice," Robin said. "That new girl can really kick."

"She is not so good," said Marty. But Marty had a sick feeling in her stomach.

Marty looked back at the soccer field. That was when she saw the monster. He wasn't big but he was ugly. And he was slime green. Yuck! "Look at that!" Marty said. She pointed to the empty bleachers.

"I don't see anything," said Robin.

"In the bleachers," said Marty. "You don't see a green monster in the bleachers?"

"Monster?" said Robin. "What monster?" Robin put her hands on her hips. "Marty Milton," she said. "You are not going to scare me with some baby game." And off she marched up the street.

"Robin, wait!" called Marty, running after her. But Robin was too far ahead. Marty slowed down and looked back. The monster was following her! "Go away!" Marty shouted. She made her meanest face. The monster did not move.

Marty turned and quickly walked home. Mom met her at the door. Marty looked over her shoulder. The monster was standing on the sidewalk. Marty scooted inside.

"Quick, Mom!" she said. "Shut the door."

"Why?" asked Mom.

"Please," said Marty.

Mom gave Marty a strange look. Then she shrugged and shut the door. "Whew!" said Marty. Marty flopped into a kitchen chair.

"How was practice?" Mom asked. She gave Marty a dish of yogurt.

"OK, I guess," said Marty. "We got a new girl on the team. Her name is Kris. And boy, is she a creep!"

"Marty . . ." said Mom with a frown on her face.

"OK, OK," said Marty. "But she's not very nice."

"How do you know?" asked Mom. "You just met her."

Marty poked her peach yogurt with her spoon.

"Well," she said, "after practice, I needed to talk to Coach. But Kris kept talking to him. And talking to him!" Marty put down her spoon.

"Coach acted like I wasn't even there," she said. "Just because Kris is a good kicker." Marty got up and put her dish in the sink. Behind her, Marty heard someone chewing. She turned around. There was the monster! How did he get in here? Marty wondered. What is he eating? And why is he following me?

"Marty, are you feeling a bit jealous?" asked Mom. The monster nodded. "Me? No," said Marty. "I have to practice now."

In the backyard, Marty dropped her soccer ball onto the grass. She looked at the goal across the yard. She kicked the ball. Running after it, she kicked the ball again. It shot into the goal net.

"Yes!" yelled Marty.

Marty picked up the ball and spun it around.

"Just wait until the game on Saturday," she said. "Coach will see. Everyone will see. I'm just as good as Kris. In fact, I'm better."

Someone smacked his lips. Marty looked behind her. Standing by the fence was the monster. He was eating again. He was eating Marty's words! He was grabbing them right out of the air and eating them! Marty stared. How did the monster do that? She put her hands over her eyes. But then she peeked. Ugh! Was the monster really getting bigger?

On Saturday, Marty's team lost.

"Losing is hard," said Coach. "But you all tried and you played a good game."

Not me, thought Marty. I did not play a good game. I kicked the ball out of bounds so many times. I did not score once. But Kris scored. Kris scored our only goal. Marty looked up at the empty bleachers. The green monster was there. He waved at her. Marty frowned. Could this day get any worse?

“Oh, no,” said Robin to Marty. “Here comes my brother.”

Robin’s older brother, Josh, socked Robin on the arm.

“Too bad about the game,” he said. “Maybe you will win next time. Kris is a great kicker. Ask her to teach you, Marty.”

Marty felt her face get hot. She wanted to cry, but not in front of Josh.

Marty walked away. She could hear the monster following her.

“Marty, wait!” called Robin.

Marty stopped. She stared at her shoes.

“Don’t listen to Josh,” said Robin. “You are a good kicker. And you are my best friend.” Marty smiled. Then Kris walked by with Coach. Marty stopped smiling.

“Kris thinks she is the queen of the soccer field,” said Marty. She could hear the monster chewing noisily again. She put her hands over her ears and ran to the car where Mom was waiting.

On Sunday after lunch, Marty helped Mom load the dishwasher. "We heard about Joseph in Sunday school today," said Marty. "I think his coat of many colors must have been beautiful. But his brothers were so mean to him."

"They were jealous," said Mom.

"Jealous?" asked Marty. She almost dropped a dish. The monster laughed and stuck out his tongue.

"Mom, have you ever been jealous?" asked Marty.

"Sure," said Mom. "Most people are jealous sometimes."

"How do you feel when you are jealous?" asked Marty.

"When I am jealous, I feel mad and sad," said Mom. "Like someone has taken my place. Sometimes I feel like a monster is following me."

Marty's mouth fell open.

"Oh, Mom!" she said. "Ever since Kris came, I've felt like a monster is following me! I wish Kris had never come. Before she came, I was the best. Kris is the best kicker now."

"But you are the only Marty Milton," said Mom. "God made only one of you. And God wants to help you be the very best you ever could be."

Mom put her hand gently on Marty's shoulder. "Marty, would you like to talk to God about this?" she asked.

The monster yelled, "No, no!"

Marty looked at the monster. Then she looked at Mom. "Oh yes, yes!" Marty said. "Please, let's pray." She bowed her head.

By the next soccer practice, Marty had a plan. The whistle blew. "OK, that's it for today," said Coach. "Good practice."

Marty turned to Robin. "I am going to ask her," said Marty. "Come with me." Marty and Robin walked over to Kris.

"Hey, Kris," said Marty. "Robin is coming to my house tomorrow to practice. Do you want to come, too?"

Kris smiled a big smile. "Sure!" she said. "Come with me to ask my mom."

The three girls walked to Kris's car. "We are going to have a great team," said Robin.

Marty nodded. She thought about the monster. Was he still there? She looked back at the bleachers and grinned. The monster was still there, but he was smaller. A lot smaller. He was shrinking even at she looked.

CHARLIE THE CHAMP

written by Clare Mishica
illustrated by Kathleen Estes

Whack!! Charlie's bat hit the ball. Up, up, up went the ball, over the fence and over the apple trees. "Woo! Woo! Woo!" shouted Charlie's team, the Rhinos. "Charlie is a champ!"

Charlie's sister, Kate, ran after the ball. She found it in the long grass. "Throw it here," the pitcher called. Kate threw the ball with all her might. She threw it right into the frog pond.

"What are you doing?" Charlie shouted to Kate. "Let the Cheetahs get the ball. You are a Rhino. We are batting. Now come and sit down." So Kate sat on the bench and watched.

Todd hit a single. He ran to first base. Chad hit a double. He ran to second base. Jasmine hit a triple. She ran to third base. Zach hit a fly ball. Up, up, up it went, but an outfielder caught the ball.

"That is two outs," said Charlie.

Then Kate stepped up to bat. Swish! "Strike one!" called the ump. Swish! "Strike two!" called the ump. Swish! "Strike three!" called the ump. "You are out."

"That is three outs," said the Cheetahs. "Now we are up to bat." Charlie and the Rhinos took the field.

"You go in right field," Charlie told Kate. "If you get the ball, throw it to me."

Poof! Poof! Poof! Poof! Kate blew four fuzzy dandelions into the air. But the ball did not come to Kate.

Then Kate found a fat caterpillar creeping up the apple tree. She let it crawl up her finger while she waited for the ball. But the ball did not come.

Then Kate started to make a daisy chain, and whack! The Cheetahs' batter hit the ball. Hard. Up, up, up went the ball, over the fence and over the apple trees. Kate did not see the ball coming. But she did hear Charlie. "Get the ball!" he shouted.

Kate jumped up. She grabbed the ball. She put her arm way back. She threw the ball with all her might. She threw it right into the bushes. "I will get the ball," said Kate. She found the ball and a bee's nest! Bzzzzz . . . Out the bees buzzed. "Run!" shouted Kate. And everyone ran home.

At the next game, Charlie hit two home runs. "Woo! Woo! Woo!" shouted the Rhinos. "Charlie is a champ!" Kate struck out.

In the field, Kate missed a pop-up. The ball landed on her toes. Her big toe hurt for two days.

At the game after that, Charlie hit three home runs. Kate struck out and threw the ball into the frog pond. Again.

The next day, when it was time for baseball practice, Charlie told Kate to watch the circus on TV. Then he tiptoed toward the back door. But Kate found him. "The circus show is over," she said.

"Why don't you make a picture?" said Charlie. "Go get my markers. They are in my room."

Kate went to get the markers. Charlie tiptoed out of the house and into the garage. He got his bat and mitt. He tiptoed out. He tiptoed right into his big brother, Ross. "Time for baseball practice?" asked Ross. "Where is Kate?"

"Oh, Ross," said Charlie. "Baseball is no fun when Kate comes. She can't hit the ball. And she never, ever, throws the ball straight."

Ross laughed. "That is just how you used to play," he said.

"Not me," said Charlie. "I am Charlie the Champ. I can hit a home run."

"But you could not hit a home run last year," said Ross. "I helped you learn to hit. I helped you learn to throw. I helped you every day."

"You are right," said Charlie.

"And now you are a baseball champ," said Ross. "But there is one way you can be a real champ."

"How?" asked Charlie.

"Think about it," said Ross.

Charlie thought about it. He thought about Ross. Ross had helped him a lot. He thought about Kate. He had not helped Kate at all. Charlie ran back inside the house. "Kate!" called Charlie. "Get you mitt!"

"Is it time for our game?" asked Kate.

"No," said Charlie. "It is time to practice."

Charlie showed Kate how to hold the bat. He showed her how to hit. But when Charlie pitched to Kate, she still struck out.

"That's OK," said Charlie. "We will try again tomorrow."

All week, Charlie and Kate practiced throwing and catching, batting and bunting, running and jumping, tagging and sliding. On Friday, Kate finally hit the ball. "Way to go!" yelled Charlie.

At the next game, Kate stepped up to the plate with a smile on her face. "Easy out!" yelled the Cheetahs.

Kate did not listen. Kate swung the bat with all her might. Whack! Up, up, up went the ball, over the fence and into the apple trees.

"Woo! Woo! Woo! shouted the Rhinos. "It is a home run. Kate hit a home run!"

And even though everyone was cheering for Kate, Charlie felt like a real champ!